Inspiring Stories from
PANCHATANTRA

Compiled by

'KUNWAR' ANIL KUMAR

MANOJ PUBLICATIONS

CONTENTS

Manoj Publications
761, Main Road Burari, Delhi-110084
Phone : 27611116, 27611349
Fax : 27611546, *Mobile :* 9868112194
E-mail : manojpublications @vsnl.net
Website : www.manojpublications.com
ISBN : 81-8133-404-3

Showroom :

1583-84, Dariba Kalan,
Chandani Chowk, Delhi-6
Phone : 23262174, 23268216
Mobile : 9818753569

Printers :
Jain Offset Printers

THE GOLDEN BIRDS AND THE GOLDEN SWANS

ONCE upon a time there lived a mighty king in the state of Rajasthan. He had a beautiful palace in the 'city of lakes'. One such lake surrounded his palace with a beautiful garden around it. There were many golden swans living at this lake. These golden swans used to shed golden feathers everyday. The king collected all such feathers and kept them in his state treasury.

Once, a huge golden bird came flying to the lake. He perched on the branch of a tall tree standing near the lake. He liked the lake's sweet water very much and decided to make the lake his home. But the swans didn't tolerate his presence there.

"Who're you?" the golden swans asked the golden bird. "What for have you come here? Better get out, otherwise, we'll beat you."

"Why? Is this not king's palace ground?" the golden bird asked.

"It was," the swans replied, "but, not now. We've bought this place from the king. Now even he can't enter the lake area without our permission. Do you understand? Now get out of this place."

The golden bird then flew to the palace garden and waited for the king to arrive to take a walk in the garden. Soon the king came there with his armed guards and began to take morning stroll in the garden.

The golden bird then flew to the king and said to him, "Your Majesty, I came to your beautiful kingdom from a foreign land. I wanted to settle here. But, the golden swans already living here drove me out of the lake. They are very arrogant. They say that they have bought the lake from you and now even you can't enter the lake without their permission. I advised them not to speak ill, but still they talk arrogantly."

Hearing this the king became very angry. He ordered his soldiers to go to the lake and kill all those arrogant golden swans, because they had spoken ill of him.

However an elderly swan guarding the lake saw the soldiers coming towards the lake with naked swords in their hands. He was quick to know what was going to happen. He called a gathering of golden swans and said to them, "Let's fly to some other lake. The king's soldiers are coming to kill us."

Acting upon his good advice, all the golden swans took to their wings, well before the king's soldiers arrived there to kill them.

It was a great loss for the king, for he believed a stranger blindly and ordered his soldiers to kill the golden swans. Now he would never get those golden feathers. The golden swans too had to abandon the beautiful royal lake because of their arrogant nature.

The king became so dejected to lose those golden swans that he asked the golden bird to find a different home for himself somewhere else.

Moral—*Never act hastily believing a stranger's words. It's also undesirable to be as arrogant as the golden swans were.*

THE OLD GREEDY CRANE

THERE was an old crane, who lived by a lake. He was so old that he could not arrange for his food. The fish swam around him, but he was so weak that he could not catch them.

One day, he was very hungry. He hadn't had anything to eat for days together. In total dejection he sat on the bank of the lake and began weeping. A crab who was passing by, heard him crying and asked him for the reason.

All of a sudden, he hit upon an idea. He asked the crab to have patience and allow him some time to overcome his emotion. The crab consoled him and became silent. Meanwhile, the crane pretended to have overcome his emotions and began saying in a sad tone, "Perhaps, you are not aware of the future of the aquatic animals of this lake. They will soon die without water."

"What!" the crab exclaimed.

"Yes", the crane said. "A fortune teller has told me that very soon this lake will go dry and all the creatures living in it will die. This thought of impending doom has sunken my heart with grief." After a pause, the crane continued, "There is another lake at some distance from here. All the big creatures like crocodiles, tortoises, frogs etc. can travel upto that lake, but I am worried about those, who cannot travel by land, like fish. They will die without water. This is the reason why I am so sad. I want to help them."

All the creatures in the lake were dumbstruck to know the future of the lake but they became very happy to know that the crane was ready to help them.

"There is a big lake, full of water, a few miles away from here. I'll carry such helpless creatures on my back", said the crane, "and put them safely in the big lake."

Everyone in the lake agreed to this proposal. Now the crane started carrying one creature at a time, on his back. First, he started with fish and carried them on his back; but, instead of taking them to the big lake, he took them to a nearby hill and ate them.

And in this way, the crane ate a large number of fish everyday. Within a few days, he regained his health and became stout.

One day, the crab said to the crane, "Friend, you seem to have forgotten me. I thought, I would be the first one to be carried to the big lake, but I have a feeling that I have been completely ignored."

"No, I haven't forgotten you", said the crane cunningly. He was tired of eating fish everyday. He wanted to have a change. So he said to the crab, "Come my friend. Sit on my back."

The crab gladly sat on the crane's back and the crane flew towards the big lake.

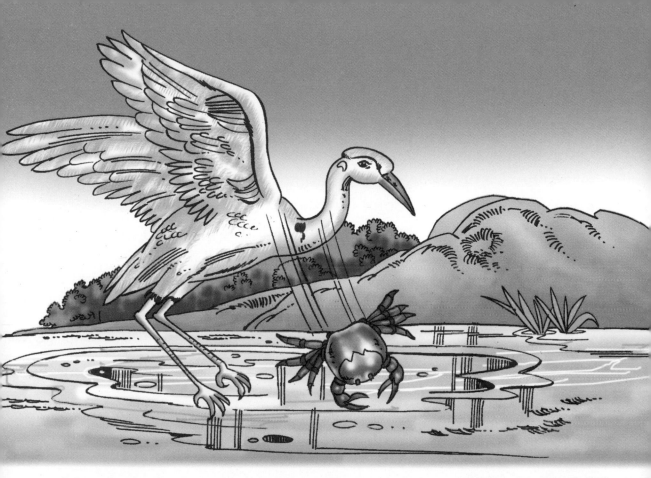

"How far is the lake now?" the crab asked. The crane thought that the crab was quite an innocent creature. He would never know his evil plans. So, he said angrily, "You fool, do you think I am your servant? There is no other lake around here. I made this plan in order to be able to eat you all. Now you too be prepared to die."

But the crab didn't loose his senses. He quickly grabbed the long neck of the crane with his sharp claws and told him to return to the old lake. He threatened to cut the crane's neck into two, if he didn't obey him.

The crane was left with no choice, but to return to the old lake. On reaching the lake the crab immediately jumped off the back of the crane. Then he told all the other creatures about the crane's misdeeds. This made the creatures very angry. They attacked the crane and killed him.

Moral—*Never be greedy.*

THE FOOLISH JACKAL

THERE lived two big bulls in a village. The village was situated near a thick forest. Once on some issue the bulls began fighting fiercely on the outskirts of the village. They would keep their horns locked with each other for hours together. Then, they would walk back a little and again run into each other dashing their heads together. They engaged themselves in such a fierce fighting that they badly injured themselves and soon blood started oozing from their heads. But they didn't stop fighting.

A jackal, who had been watching this bloody fight throughout from behind the thick bushes, saw the blood of the bulls dropping on to the ground. He came out of the bushes to lick it.

Without a second thought, the jackal made his way between those two bulls and started licking the blood.

While he was still busy licking the blood happily, the bulls again retracted themselves to a few steps and then rammed fiercely into each other. They dashed their heads together. The poor jackal got crushed between their heads. His stomach burst with a loud noise and he died instantaneously.

Moral—*Never loose yours senses out of greed.*

LONG, long ago, there lived a magic bird by the name of Sindhuka in a thick forest. It laid golden eggs.

Once a fowler came to the forest. While hunting, he came near the tree in which lived the magic bird. He saw the bird laying golden eggs. He caught the bird in his net and returned home. But he was afraid of keeping the bird in his captivity. He thought that the magic bird would lay him golden eggs. Soon he would be rich. The king might think that he became rich by stealing others' money. He might send him to jail. So it was better that he himself presented the magic bird to the king.

Thinking thus, the fowler presented the magic bird to the king. The king was very happy to have such a magic bird. He ordered his servants to take care of the bird, so that it laid more and more golden eggs.

But the attendants said to the king, "Your Majesty, this is all a hoax. How can a bird lay golden eggs?" This created doubts in the mind of the king. He ordered his attendants to release the bird in the woods.

The attendants, thereafter, released the bird in the woods.

The bird flew in the sky and thought to itself, "This seems to be a fool's kingdom. The fowler knew that I laid golden eggs, but he gifted me to the king. The king in turn gave me to the attendants to release me in the woods. The attendants too didn't ever believe in my magical qualities and spoke to the king against me. And the biggest fool of them was I, who landed into the fowler's net."

Moral—*Take a decision after verifying the facts.*

ONCE upon a time there lived a big bull in a village. The village was situated near a lake. One day, when the bull felt thirsty, he started walking towards the lake.

There was a tiny mouse living in the same village. The mouse was sitting by the side of the lake and basking in the sun. The bull who was going to drink water from the lake stepped on the tail of the mouse. The mouse squeaked in pain. He looked at his tail. It was completely crushed. 'This foolish bull has crushed my tail. I'll bite this bull to death.' The mouse said to himself and jumped on to the bull's back and started biting him with his sharp teeth. The bull didn't feel any pain. He was rather unaware of the presence of a little mouse on his back.

After sometime the mouse was tired of biting the bull. Seeing no reaction, he jumped off the bull's back and stood before him blocking his way. The bull looked at the mouse and asked, "Why do you block my way? Get out of my path, otherwise, you'll be crushed."

"You've already done it," said the mouse angrily. He showed his tail to the bull and said, "I bit you all over your back. Didn't you feel any pain?."

The bull was surprised to listen to this. He laughed and replied, "Did I really stamp on your tail and did you really bite me all over my body? I never realised both. However I'm sorry, if it really happened?

The mouse was left speechless to hear the bull's answer. He thought to himself that it was quite useless to argue with that thick skinned animal. The mouse felt very much disgusted and went to his home crying in pain.

Moral—*It's no use arguing with a stupid person.*

THE FOX AND THE ELEPHANT

THERE lived a huge elephant in a dense jungle. He was cruel and arrogant by nature. He roamed freely in the jungle, pulling down small trees and branches. Those animals who lived in the trees were very much afraid of this elephant. When he pulled down the trees and tore off the branches, many a nests with eggs and nestlings came down crashing on the ground and got destroyed. His movement in the jungle created an all round havoc. Even the tigers and lions kept themselves at a safe distance from this rogue. In his ruthless march in the jungle, many holes of the foxes were trampled. This led to dissatisfaction among the foxes and among the other animals alike. Many of them wanted to kill the elephant. But this task was very difficult, because of his huge size.

"He is so huge", said the foxes amongst themselves. "It's nearly impossible to kill him."

Then a meeting of all the foxes was called. In the meeting this rather impossible task was assigned to a very cunning fox to perform. The fox, before executing his plan studied the elephant's behaviour for many days.

One day, the fox went to meet the elephant and said to him, "Your Highness. It's urgent to talk to you. It's a matter of life and death for us."

The elephant trumpeted at his highest pitch and asked, "Who're you and why do you want to see me?"

"Your Highness", said the fox. "I'm the representative of the whole of the animal community. We want to make you our supreme head—the king. Kindly accept our offer."

The elephant lifted his trunk with great pride and asked for details.

The fox further explained, "I've come to take you with me. The coronation ceremony will take place in the middle of the jungle, where thousands of animals have already gathered and are chanting holy mantras."

The elephant was very glad to hear this. He had always cherished a dream to become a king. He thought that the coronation ceremony will be a matter of pride to him. He readied himself hurriedly to accompany the fox to the deep jungle.

"Come, Your Highness," said the fox. "Follow me."

The fox led the elephant to some imaginary spot of ceremony. On their way, they had to walk through a swampy area by the side of a pond. The fox being light bodied, crossed the small swampy patch without any difficulty. The elephant too walked on it, but being heavily built, he got stuck into the swamp. The more he tried to come out of the swamp, the more he went deep into it. He became scared and called out the fox, "Dear friend. Please help me. I'm sinking in the mud. What'll happen to my coronation now. Call your other friends also to help me."

"I'm not going to save you", said the fox. "You deserved this treatment. You know, how cruel you have been to other animals all along. You pulled down branches of trees mercilessly, without caring for the eggs and for the lives of the nestlings. You knew everything, but remained indifferent. You trampled upon the burrows of the foxes. You saw our siblings being crushed under your heavy feet. You saw us crying, begging for mercy; but nothing bothered you. And now you are begging for your life? I am sorry to tell you that though, your coronation couldn't take place, but your cremation will definitely take place." And the fox left.

The elephant couldn't come out of the swamp and died there.

Moral—_Even a tyrant has to meet his doom._

❏ ❏

THREE FISH AND THE FISHERMEN

LONG, long ago, there lived three fish with their families in a pond. Their names were Anagatavidhata, Pratyutpannamati and Yadbhavishya. Anagatavidhata was very practical. She always planned her actions in advance. Pratyutpannamati too was practical and always tendered good advices to her elder sister Anagatavidhata. Yadbhavishya, the youngest of them all, loved to laze around only. She didn't like to work at all.

One day, some fishermen came to the pond. One of them said, "This is the pond I was telling you about. There are many fish in this pond. Let's come here tomorrow and catch all of them."

Anagatavidhata overheard the fishermen's talk. She gathered all the fish in the pond and narrated to them what she had heard about. She said, "It's better that we move out of here to some other safer pond. Our life will, at least, be safe." Everybody agreed to this proposal including Pratyutpannamati. But Yadbhavishya said, "Why should we run like cowards from this pond. Let the fishermen come. We'll see to it together that we're not caught in the net. Besides, who knows the fishermen would really turn up here. After all, everyone has to die one day. So why be afraid of death."

But Anagatavidhata and Pratyutpannamati didn't agree with Yadbhavishya's ideas. They moved out to another pond with their families to live with their other near and dear ones.

The next morning, the fishermen came to the pond. They cast their net in the pond and trapped Yadbhavishya and her family alongwith a large number of other fish living in the pond.

Moral—*Always plan your future intelligently.*

❑❑

THE JACKAL AND THE DRUM

ONCE upon a time, in a jungle there lived a jackal by the name of Gomaya. One day, he was very hungry and was wandering in search of food. While wandering, he came across a battle field. There he saw a big drum lying under a tree. When the wind blew, a tender branch grown at the root of the tree struck the drum producing sound of a drum beat. The jackal examined the drum from all sides and then beat the drum with his front paws. The drum made a sound. Now the jackal thought that there might be some other small animal inside the drum and that would make a very tasty meal for him. But he found the top of the drum too tough to tear off.

The jackal thought of a plan and began to beat the drum with both his front paws. The sound of drumbeat filled the whole jungle. A leopard who was attracted towards the sound of the drum, came near it. The jackal said to the leopard, "Your Majesty, there is some animal hiding inside the drum. Since you have sharp claws and strong teeth, you can tear off the top of the drum and catch your prey inside the drum."

The leopard was himself hungry. So he hit the top of the drum with his heavy paws. The drum burst with a sound, but there was no animal inside. The drum was empty.

Seeing the empty drum, the leopard became very angry and said to the jackal, "You have wasted my time. There is no food inside the drum. So I will kill and eat you."

The leopard pounced upon the jackal and killed and ate him.

Moral—*Greed is always harmful.*

BEWARE OF MEAN FRIENDS

THERE in a deep jungle, lived a lion by the name of Madotkata. He had three selfish friends—a jackal, a crow and a wolf. They had become friendly with the lion, because he was the king of the forest. They were always at the service of the lion and obeyed him to meet their selfish ends.

Once, a camel got disorientated in the jungle while grazing and went astray. He tried hard to find his way out, but could not succeed.

In the meantime, these three friends of the lion saw the camel, wandering in a confused manner.

"He doesn't seem to come from our forest", said the jackal to his friends. "Let's kill and eat him."

"No", said the wolf. "It's a big animal. Let's go and inform our king, the lion."

"Yes, this is a good idea", said the crow. "We can have our share of flesh after the king kills the camel."

Having decided upon this the three went to meet the lion.

"Your Majesty", said the jackal, "a camel from some other forest has entered into your kingdom without your permission. His body is full of delicious flesh. He may prove to be our best meal. Let's kill him".

Hearing the advice of his friends, the lion roared in anger and said, "What're you talking about? The camel has walked into my kingdom for the sake of his safety. We should give him shelter and not kill him. Go and bring him to me."

The three became very disheartened to hear the lion's words. But they were helpless. So having no alternative, they went to the camel and told him about the wishes of the lion who wanted to meet him and have dinner with him.

The camel was terribly frightened to learn the awkward proposal. Thinking that his last moment had arrived and soon he would be killed by the king of the forest, he resigned himself to the mercy of his fate and went to see the lion in his den.

However, the lion was very happy to see him. He talked to him sweetly and assured him of all the safety in the forest, so long as he stayed there. The camel was simply astonished and was very happy to hear the lion's words. He began living with the jackal, the wolf and the crow.

But once, bad luck struck the lion. One day, while he was hunting for food with his friends, he had a fight with a huge elephant. The fight was so fierce that all his three friends fled the spot in panic. The lion was badly wounded in the fight. Although, he killed the elephant, but he himself became incapable of hunting for his food. Day after day, he had to go without food. His friends too had to starve for days together as they depended entirely on the lion's prey for their food. But the camel grazed around happily.

One day the three friends—the jackal, the wolf and the crow approached the lion and said, "Your Majesty, you're becoming weak day after day. We can't see you in this pitiable condition. Why don't you kill the camel and eat him?"

"No", roared the lion, "he is our guest. We can't kill him. Don't make such suggestions to me in future."

But the jackal, the wolf and the crow had set their evil eyes on the camel. They met together once again and hatched a plan to kill the camel.

They went to the camel and said, "My dear friend, you know our king has had nothing to eat for the last so many days. He cannot go hunting due to his wounds and physical infirmity. Under these circumstances, it becomes our duty to sacrifice ourselves to save the life of our king. Come, let us go to our king and offer our bodies for his food."

Innocent camel didn't understand their plot. He nodded and consented in favour of their proposal.

All the four reached the den of the lion. The jackal said to the lion, "Your Majesty, despite our best of efforts, we couldn't find a prey."

First, the crow came forward and offered himself for the noble cause.

"So, you can eat me and assuage your hunger", said the crow to the lion.

"Your body is too small", said the jackal. "How can the king assuage his hunger by eating you?"

The jackal offered his own body to the lion for food. He said, "Your Majesty, I offer myself. It's my solemn duty to save your life."

"No", said the wolf, "you too are too small to assuage the hunger of our King. I offer myself for this noble task. Kill me and eat me, Your Majesty," he said lying prostrate before the lion.

But the lion didn't kill any of them.

The camel was standing nearby and watching all that was going on there. He also decided to go forward and fulfil the formality.

He stepped forward and said, "Your Majesty, why not me! You're my friend. A friend in need is a friend indeed. Please kill me and eat my flesh to assuage your hunger."

The lion liked the camel's idea. Since, the camel himself had offered his body for food, his conscience won't prick and the jackal had already told the lion about the intense desire of the camel to sacrifice himself for the welfare of the king. He immediately pounced upon the camel and tore him into pieces. The lion and his friends had a good and sumptuous meal for days together.

Moral—*Beware of people, who become friendly to fulfil their evil desires. They talk sweetly, but in reality, they are never trustworthy.*

❑❑

THE FROG AND THE SERPENT

THERE lived a frog king by the name of Gangadatta, in a deep well. His subjects and other relatives too lived in the same well. The relatives had an evil eye on his throne and often created problems for the king frog. In order to disrupt the smooth working of the kingdom, and with a view to cause impediments, they hatched a plan with the connivance of a minister of the kingdom and soon there was a revolt against the king frog. The king frog somehow managed to subdue the revolt, but he was very unhappy. He took a vow to take a revenge and teach them the lesson of their life. One day, he came out of the well with the help of iron chains hanging on the walls of the well. He headed straight towards the hole of a big black serpent, which he had seen earlier.

Keeping himself at a considerably safe distance, king frog called out to the serpent. The serpent was surprised to hear a frog calling him. He came out of the hole.

"I wish to be your friend", said the king frog.

"But we are born enemies," replied the serpent. "How's it possible?"

"I will make it possible. I have a proposal," said king frog. He spoke to the serpent about his plan and told him that he was bent upon teaching his relatives a lesson. "I want to punish them. I will take you to the well and in the process you can eat them all."

"Is it a dry well?" asked the serpent.

"There is not much water in it", said the king frog. "However, you needn't worry. There is a nice hole in the wall of the well, a little above the water level. You can eat my relative frogs and retire into it to take rest."

"Okay, lead me to the well. I'll teach your relatives a lesson", said the serpent hissing loudly.

The king frog took the serpent to his well and said, "Here live my relatives and rebels. You can eat them all, but please spare my near and dear ones."

"All right," said the serpent and entered the well followed by the king frog. There he started eating the frogs, one by one, as and when pointed out by the king frog. Soon all the enemies of the king frog were eaten up by the serpent.

Now it was the turn of the king frog and his family. The serpent said to the king frog, "As you see, I've finished all your relatives and rebels. I've eaten your disloyal minister also. Now I've nothing to eat except you and your family."

King frog realised his folly. He had befriended his enemy to achieve his own selfish ends and settle his score with his enemies. The king frog felt as if the god of death was in his hot persuit. He, somehow, managed to gather some courage and said to the serpent, "No problem. I'll visit some other wells and ponds and persuade the frogs living there to resettle themselves in this empty well. Once they are in here, you can feast on them with ease."

"That's, good", the serpent became happy. "Do it soon. I'm hungry."

Both the king frog and his wife came out of the well and took to their heels, never to return to the same well again.

Moral—*Never look to an enemy for help.*

THE GOLDEN GOAT

THERE lived a golden goat in a deep forest. He was as big as a pony and as strong as a bull. He had two pointed horns. His golden hair shone like burning flames in the bright sunlight. Even lions and tigers were afraid of facing this goat.

Once a lion saw the goat on the outskirts of a village, eating vegetable leaves in the garden of a farmer. The farmer seeing the goat in his garden beat him with sticks. The lion thought to himself, "How can a grass eating animal be stronger than I."

When the goat came out of the vegetable garden bleating after being beaten by the farmer, the lion pounced upon him. He killed the goat and ate it.

Moral—*Keep your eating habits and personal traits a secret.*

WHEN THE LION CAME BACK TO LIFE

LONG, long ago, there lived four friends in a village. Three of them were very learned, but they absolutely lacked in common sense. The fourth one, although not much learned, had a lot of common sense. He, at least, knew what was good and what was bad and was practical to quite an extent.

Once the three learned friends decided to travel to far off towns and cities in order to make their fortune. They were not ready to take their fourth friend with them, because he was not learned, but ultimately agreed to do so, considering that he was their childhood friend.

Soon the four friends set out on a long journey. They walked from one city to another, looking for an opportunity to amass wealth. Once, while they were passing through a dense forest, they came across a heap of bones lying under a tree.

One of the learned friends observed the bones and said, "Here is a fine opportunity to test our knowledge. These are the bones of a lion. Let's bring this lion back to life."

Then he assembled all the bones together to make it into a skeleton of a lion and chanted some mantras.

The second learned man chanted some other mantras and put skin, flesh and blood into the skeleton. Now it looked like a lion, but lifeless.

And the third learned man got up to do the final act of putting life into the lifeless body of the animal.

As he started chanting the mantras, the fourth friend shouted, "Stop! please don't do this. It might prove dangerous to bring this beast back to life."

"Shut up, you fool," said all the three friends. "What do you know in the field of learning and knowledge. Better you keep your mouth shut."

"Wait a minute please," said the fourth friend and quickly climbed up a nearby tall tree.

His three friends laughed. They put life into the lifeless body of the lion.

As soon as the huge lion came back to life, he roared loudly and killed all the three learned men. He ate their flesh and disappeared behind the thick bushes.

Moral—*Knowledge without common sense is useless.*

THE CUNNING SNAKE

THERE lived a brown snake by the name of Mandvishya near a pond. The pond was full of frogs—big and small. They were all leading a happy life under the good rule of their king frog. The big brown snake had become old and weak and could no more catch his prey easily for his meals. So he decided to play a ruse upon the frogs. One day, he went to the pond and lay there as if he was suffering from illness. After sometime, the king frog happened to come out of water. He saw the brown snake lying by the side of the pond in a pitiable condition. When he asked for the reason in a frightened tone, the snake said, "A week before, I bit the son of a pundit by mistake, because he had tried to kill me with a stick. He died immediately. Now the pundit has cursed me. According to his curse, I'll have to serve the frogs and have to eat whatever they offer me for food. So, I'm here to serve you."

The king frog and his ministers were delighted to hear this. Other frogs also gathered around the snake. Many of the minister frogs and the king frog too jumped on to the back of the brown snake to have a joy ride. The brown snake swam round the pond with all the frogs riding on his back.

The next day also the frogs rode over the entire length of the snake's back. The snake swam in the pond. Soon the king frog realised that the snake's movement had slowed down. When he asked for the reason, the brown snake said, "Your Majesty, due to constant swimming and non-availability of food, I've gone weak. I can't move any more now."

The king frog, thinking that in view of the snake's physical weakness, he might not be able to have joy rides in future, allowed the snake to eat a few frogs.

The brown snake, thus, started eating the frogs easily, one by one. One day, there were no frogs left in the pond, except the king frog. So the snake spoke to the king frog. "I can't remain hungry anymore. There are no frogs now left in the pond except you. So, please excuse me for eating you." And the brown snake attacked the frog with a lightening speed and ate him also.

Moral—*Never trust your enemy.*